FUNNYBONES

Dinosaur Dreams

ALLAN AHLBERG • ANDRÉ AMSTUTZ

PUFFIN

In a dark dark street
there is a tall tall house.
In the tall tall house
there is a deep deep cellar.
In the deep deep cellar
there is a cosy cosy bed.
And in the cosy cosy bed . . .

. . . three skeletons are dreaming.
The big skeleton is dreaming
about dinosaurs.
"I knew dinosaurs could run," he says
(in his dream).
"I never knew they had roller skates!"

Suddenly, the big skeleton is chased
by a very big dinosaur.
"You can't scare me," he says.
"You're just a dream."
"Grr!" growls the dinosaur.
"Help!" shouts the big skeleton.
And he runs away.

The little skeleton is dreaming
about dinosaurs too.
"I knew dinosaurs could swim," he says.
"I never knew they had armbands!"

Suddenly, the little skeleton is chased
by a little dinosaur.
"You can't scare me," he says.
"You're just a fossil."
"Grr!" growls the dinosaur.
"Help!" shouts the little skeleton.
And *he* runs away.

The dog skeleton is also dreaming
about dinosaurs.
Suddenly, into his dream
comes the little skeleton
chased by a little dinosaur,
and the big skeleton
chased by a big dinosaur.

The dog skeleton
barks at the dinosaurs:
"Woof!"
And *he* chases *them*!
"Hooray!" says the big skeleton.
"Hooray!" says the little skeleton.
"Give that dog a bone!"

The dinosaurs run away.

The dinosaurs swim away.

The dinosaurs fly away.

The dinosaurs *hide* away.

But the dog skeleton finds them
and chases them again.
The dinosaurs don't look
where they are going.
Suddenly, there is a great big crash
and a very great big . . .

For some reason
(remember, this is a dream),

the big skeleton
and the little skeleton

put the dinosaur bones
together again.

They make the biggest dinosaur
the world has ever seen . . .

. . . and *it* chases them!

At last the big skeleton
and the little skeleton wake up.
They rub their eyes
and scratch their skulls.
They talk about their dreams.

"I had a dream about dinosaurs,"
says the big skeleton.
"You were in it."
"No, I wasn't," the little skeleton says.
"You were in mine!"

After that, the big skeleton says,
"What shall we do now?"
"Let's take the dog for a walk,"
says the little skeleton.
"Good idea!" the big skeleton says.

But the dog skeleton
isn't ready for a walk.
He is still sleeping.
He has a dream bone
in his dream mouth . . .

DOGOSAURUS REX

. . . and does not want to be disturbed.